For Georgie and Conrad
 ~L.J.

For Even, with love
 ~J.M.

First published in 1997 by Magi Publications
22 Manchester Street, London W1M 5PG

This edition published 1997

Text © 1997 Linda Jennings
Illustrations © 1997 Julia Malim

Linda Jennings and Julia Malim
have asserted their rights to be identified
as the author and illustrator of this work
under the Copyright, Designs and
Patents Act, 1988.

Printed in Belgium by Proost NV, Turnhout

ISBN 1 85430 433 X

Lonely Misty

by Linda Jennings

illustrated by Julia Malim

Misty woke up, feeling cold.
All her kittens had gone to new homes
and she missed their furry bodies curled
up warmly beside her.
It was wintertime and the sky was the colour
of slate. Misty looked through the window
and saw tiny snowflakes whirling round
in the wind.

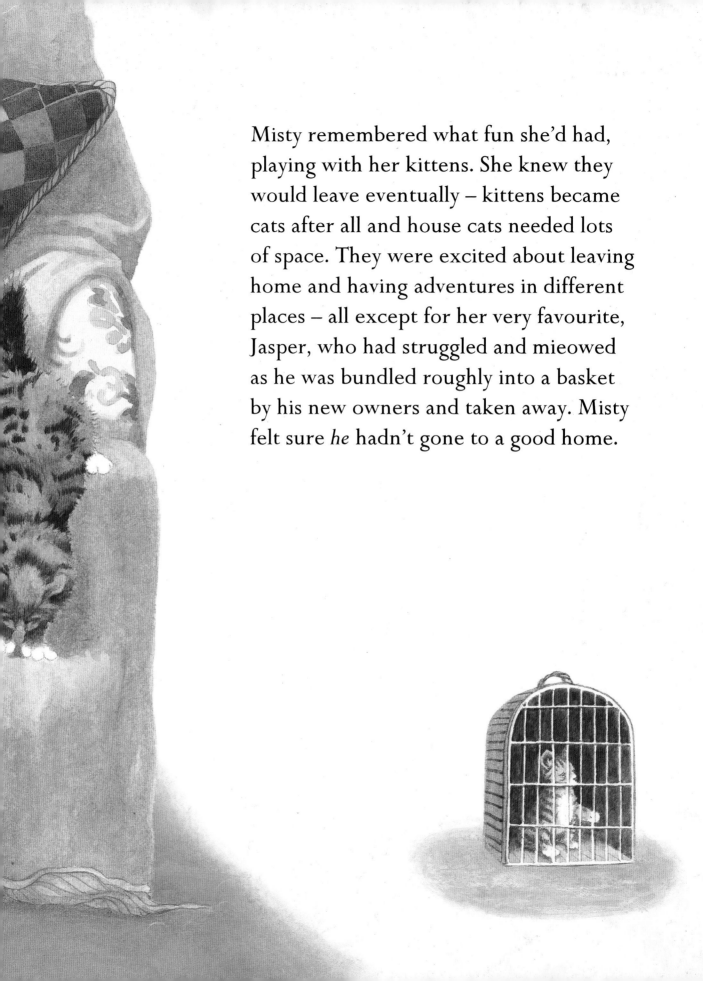

Misty remembered what fun she'd had, playing with her kittens. She knew they would leave eventually – kittens became cats after all and house cats needed lots of space. They were excited about leaving home and having adventures in different places – all except for her very favourite, Jasper, who had struggled and mieowed as he was bundled roughly into a basket by his new owners and taken away. Misty felt sure *he* hadn't gone to a good home.

In the living room everyone was busy, and didn't notice Misty at first. She wound herself round their legs and mieowed.

"Go *away*, Misty, go out and catch a mouse or something," said Dad.

Polly pushed her away, too, when Misty tried to help her wrap up a birthday present.

"Look what you've done, Misty!" she cried. "I'll *never* be ready for Sam's party now. You *are* a pest!"

Misty banged out through her cat flap.
She felt very unwanted.

Misty felt lonelier still as she crossed the silent garden and sat on the wall, watching a family of foxes playing happily in the frozen field.

Misty hadn't known her kittens would be taken away so soon. She had planned to show them the wood and the big barn beyond it before they left home. Jasper would have loved it all, she thought sadly. Misty jumped down from the wall and made her way towards the wood. She would visit the farm cats who lived in the barn, she decided.

In the wood it was very quiet and still and there was no snow under the thick pine trees. As Misty padded along the frosty path she thought she heard something. It sounded like a kitten crying. She listened again, but it was only the wind in the treetops. Misty reached the edge of the wood, where she could just see the barn across the field.

Some rough, tough farm cats lived in the barn.
They often made fun of Misty with her sleek,
well-groomed fur and her fancy ways. They didn't
understand about her loneliness at losing the kittens.
In the barn all the cats and kittens lived together.
Nobody took *them* away to new homes.
And they laughed at her when Misty told them she
had heard a kitten crying in the wood.

Misty stayed in the barn all day.
The farm cats pounced and ran about and
caught a few mice, but Misty sat shivering,
with her paws tucked under her to keep warm.
Later, all the other cats curled up together and
went to sleep. Misty felt the coldness creep
over her from eartip to toe. Though the farm
cats knew her well they didn't ask *her* to curl
up with them. She didn't belong there.

It was time for tea and Misty crept out of the barn
and into a snow-white world.
The wind blew across the fields and through the trees,
sounding again just like a lost kitten mieowing.

Though she was hungry and looked forward to a nice
warm fire, Misty knew she wouldn't be really happy.
Her catnip mouse and her scratching post wouldn't
make up for the loss of her kittens.

Down through the garden Misty padded.
Her little paws sank into the snow, making
fresh footprints. It was dark now and the
garden was full of moonshine and shadows.
One of the shadows seemed to move across
the lawn behind Misty as she went through
the cat flap.

"Ah, there you are," said Mum,
picking Misty up and giving her a hug.
"I've got some nice mince for your tea!"
Perhaps she *could* get used to life without
her kittens, thought Misty, sadly.
"What's that noise?" said Dad. "I thought
I heard something outside." He went to
open the door.

There on the step sat a wet, bedraggled
kitten with huge, frightened eyes.
Misty couldn't believe what she saw.
It was Jasper!

Misty ran up to Jasper, purring loudly.

"What a terrible sight you are!" cried Dad. "Whatever did your new owners do to make you run away like that?"

Mum put down a big saucer of food, and Misty let Jasper eat most of it.

"Can we keep him?" pleaded Polly. "*Please*, Mum."

"I don't see why not," said Mum. "Misty has seemed a bit lonely lately. Jasper will be company for her."

Later, Misty cleaned Jasper from tip to tail with
her rough tongue, as her little son told Misty how
he had run away from his horrible new home.
When he had reached the wood he had seen Misty
and followed her back.

Jasper soon fell asleep against his mother's warm side. "Tomorrow I'll show him off to the wild cats in the barn," thought Misty. Now her favourite kitten had found his way back to her she was happy at last.